WINGS

by Christopher Myers

Scholastic Press

New York

"Look at that strange boy!"

Everyone from the neighborhood

is pointing fingers and watching the sky.

"How's he doing that?"

They stretch their necks and shake their heads.

Ikarus Jackson, a new boy on my block,

is flying above the rooftops. He is

swooping and diving, looping

past people's windows and over the crowd.

I don't think he's strange.

Ikarus Jackson, the fly boy,

came to my school last Thursday.

His long, strong, proud wings followed

wherever he went.

The whole school

was staring eyes and wagging tongues.

They whispered about his wings

and his hair and his shoes.

Like they whisper about how quiet I am.

Our teacher complained

that the other kids couldn't help

but gawk and stare. He said that

Ikarus's wings blocked the blackboard

and made it hard

for the students to pay attention.

The teacher told Ikarus to leave class

until he could figure out what to do

with his wings.

He left the room quietly, dragging

his feathers behind him.

One boy snickered.

At recess the snicker grew

into a giggle and spread

across the playground.

Soon all the kids were laughing

at Ikarus Jackson's "useless" wings.

I thought that if he flew just once

everyone would stop laughing.

Ikarus looked up,

flapped his wings a couple of times,

then jumped into the air.

He swept through the schoolyard

like a slow-motion instant replay.

But the other kids were not impressed.

One girl grabbed the basketball.

A boy stuffed the handball in his pocket.

Somebody nagged,

"Nobody likes a show-off."

Their words sent Ikarus drifting

into the sky, away

from the glaring eyes

and the pointing fingers.

I waited for them

to point back at me

as I watched Ikarus

float farther and farther away.

Walking home from school,
I knew how he felt, how lonely
he must be. Maybe I
should have said something
to those mean kids.

I ran through the streets

with my eyes to the sky,

searching the clouds for Ikarus.

He struggled
to stay in the air.
His wings drooped
and his head hung low.

He landed heavily
on the edge of a building
and sat with the pigeons.
Pigeons don't make fun of people.

A policeman passing by

blew his whistle.

"You with the wings,

come down from there!

Stay yourself on the ground.

You'll get in trouble,

you'll get hurt.'"

It seemed to me
Ikarus was already in trouble
and hurt.
Could the policeman
put him in jail for flying,
for being too different?

When the neighborhood kids saw

the policeman yelling

at him, they exploded

with laughter.

Ikarus dropped to the ground.

"Stop!" I cried. "Leave him alone."

And they did.

I called to Ikarus

and he sailed closer to me.

I told him

what someone should have long ago:

"Your flying is beautiful."

For the first time, I saw Ikarus smile.

At that moment I forgot

about the kids who had laughed

at him and me. I was just glad that

Ikarus had found his wings again.

"Look at that amazing boy!"
I called to all the people
on the street as I pointed
to my new friend Ikarus
swirling through the sky.

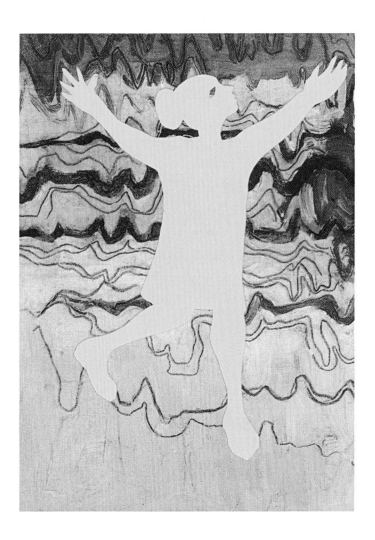

Library of Congress catalog card number: 99-087389

ISBN 978-0-590-03377-0

30 29 28 27 26 25 24 23 22 21   19 20

Printed in Malaysia   108   First edition, October 2000

Book design by David Saylor

The text type was set in 16-point Bauer Bodoni.

The artwork is cut-paper collage.

nĩ ngwedete mũno